I LOVE YOU more Than Rainbows

by **Susan E. Crites**
Illustrated by **Mark & Rosemary Jarman**

THOMAS NELSON
Since 1798

NASHVILLE   DALLAS   MEXICO CITY   RIO DE JANEIRO   BEIJING

I LOVE YOU MORE THAN RAINBOWS
© 2007 by Susan E. Crites

All rights reserved. No portion of this book may be reproduced, stored in a retrieval system, or transmitted in any form or by any means—electronic, mechanical, photocopy, recording, scanning, or other—except for brief quotations in critical reviews or articles, without the prior written permission of the publisher.

Published in Nashville, Tennessee, by Thomas Nelson. Thomas Nelson is a trademark of Thomas Nelson, Inc.

Thomas Nelson, Inc., titles may be purchased in bulk for educational, business, fund-raising, or sales promotional use. For information, please e-mail SpecialMarkets@ThomasNelson.com.

Library of Congress Cataloging-in-Publication Data
Crites, Susan E.
    I love you more than rainbows / written by Susan E. Crites ;
illustrated by Mark and Rosemary Jarman.
        p. cm.
    Summary: Rhyming text compares a parent's love to rainbows, autumn
leaves, and fresh snow.
    ISBN 978-1-4003-1089-0 (hardcover)
    ISBN 978-1-4003-8528-7 (Special Edition)
    [1. Love—Fiction. 2. Parent and child—Fiction. 3. Stories in rhyme.]
I. Jarman, Rosemary, 1970- ill. II. Jarman, Mark, 1968- ill. III. Title.
PZ8.3.C8732Ial 2007
[E]—dc22
                                                        2007016454

Printed in Singapore
07 08 09 10 11 TWP 5 4 3 2 1

For life's simple pleasures,
The people You give us to enjoy them with,
And the gift of Your perfect love,
Thank You, Lord.

For sharing your life with me, both joy and sorrow,
Always with the hope of a bright tomorrow,
My dear husband, Jeff,
I love you more than rainbows.

SC

I love you more than rainbows
and beautiful blue skies.
I love you more than buttercups
and wings of butterflies.

I love you more than a candy store
filled with all your favorite treats.
I love you more than the ocean's roar
and the sand beneath your feet.

I love you more than puppies
that romp and love to play.
I love you more than running free
on a beautiful sunny day.

I love you more than ice cream
with sprinkles on the top,
Or jumping into the pool
with a great big belly flop!

I love you more than birthday cake,
balloons, and presents, too.
I love you more than making sounds
from a farm like *oink* and *moo!*

I love you more than the circus
with all its chills and thrills.
I love you more than riding bikes
and zooming down the hills!

I love you more than a room
filled with all your favorite toys.
I love you more than the fun you have
when you make lots of noise!

I love you more than the pleasure
of a visit to the zoo,
Or the excitement of being quiet,
sneaking up, and saying, "Boo!"

I love you more than summer
    and fun under the hose.
I love you more than sledding
    and hot cocoa to warm my nose.

I love you more than a fresh snow
    so beautiful and white,
that's ready to make snowballs——
    maybe I'll take a bite!

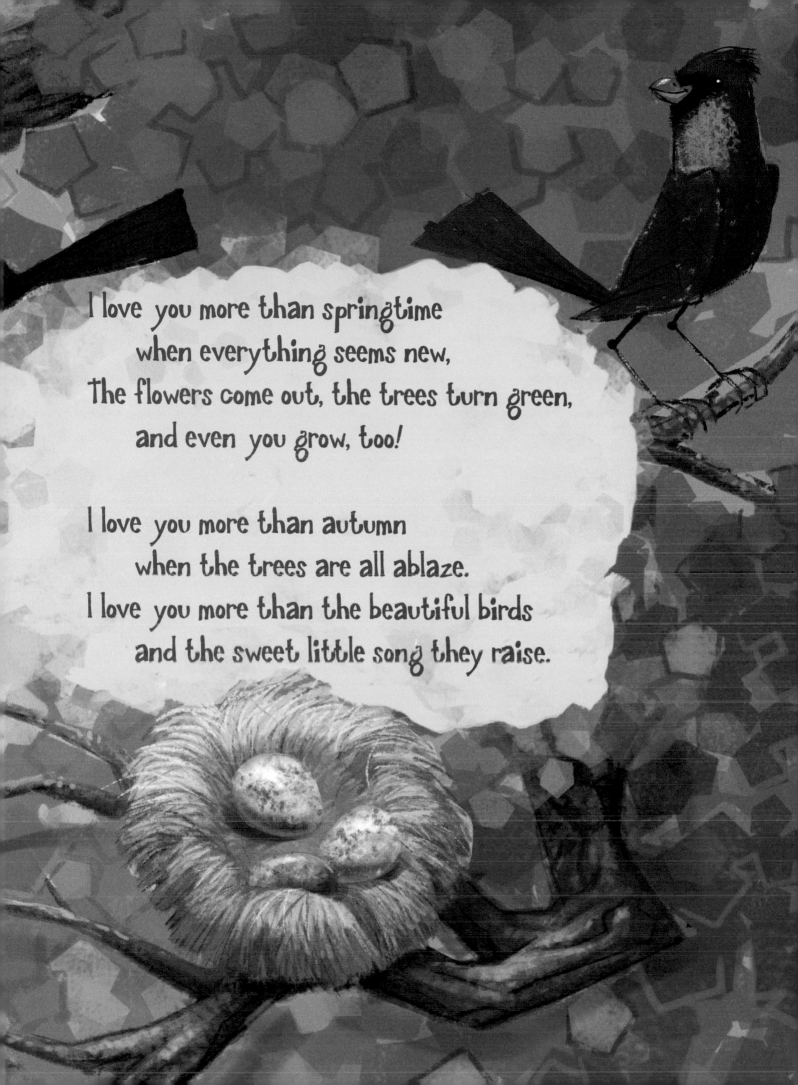

I love you more than springtime
    when everything seems new,
the flowers come out, the trees turn green,
    and even you grow, too!

I love you more than autumn
    when the trees are all ablaze.
I love you more than the beautiful birds
    and the sweet little song they raise.

I love you more than sunsets
and wishes in the sky.
I love you more than the fun you feel
when you swing like you can fly!

I love you more than raindrops
falling gently on my face,
And a sweet gentle breeze
letting all cares be erased.

So many things are nice
    and things are fun to do,
But none of them compare
    to the love I have for you.

So at night when the sky gets dark,
    and the moon begins to glow,
The stars will twinkle and deep inside
    I hope that you will know...

How much

I LOVE YOU